BLACK PANTHER

A NATION UNDER OUR FEET: PART 10

ABDOBOOKS.COM

Reinforced library bound edition published in 2021 by Spotlight,
a division of ABDO, PO Box 398166, Minneapolis, Minnesota 55439.
Spotlight produces high-quality reinforced library bound editions for
schools and libraries. Published by agreement with Marvel Characters, Inc.

Printed in the United States of America, North Mankato, Minnesota.
092020
012021

THIS BOOK CONTAINS
RECYCLED MATERIALS

© 2021 MARVEL

Library of Congress Control Number: 2020942382

Publisher's Cataloging-in-Publication Data

Names: Coates, Ta-Nehisi, author. | Sprouse, Chris; Story, Karl; Martin, Laura; Wong,
    Walden; Stelfreeze, Brian; Hanna, Scott, illustrators.
Title: A nation under our feet / by Ta-Nehisi Coates; illustrated by Chris Sprouse,
    Karl Story, Laura Martin, Walden Wong, Brian Stelfreeze and Scott Hanna.
Description: Minneapolis, Minnesota: Spotlight, 2021 | Series: Black panther
Summary: With a dramatic upheaval in Wakanda on the horizon, T'Challa knows his
    kingdom needs to change to survive, but he struggles to find balance in his
    roles as king and the Black Panther.
Identifiers: ISBN 9781532147784 (pt. 7, lib. bdg.) | ISBN 9781532147791 (pt. 8, lib.
    bdg.) | ISBN 9781532147807 (pt. 9, lib. bdg.) | ISBN 9781532147814 (pt. 10,
    lib. bdg.) | ISBN 9781532147821 (pt. 11, lib. bdg.) | ISBN 9781532147838 (pt.
    12, lib. bdg.)
Subjects: LCSH: Black Panther (Fictitious character)--Juvenile fiction. | Superheroes--
    Juvenile fiction. | Kings and rulers--Juvenile fiction. | Graphic novels--Juvenile
    fiction. | T'Challa, of Wakanda (Fictitious character)--Juvenile fiction.
Classification: DDC 741.5--dc23

Spotlight

A Division of ABDO
abdobooks.com

BLACK PANTHER

AFTER MONTHS OF PAINSTAKING RESEARCH, **KING T'CHALLA** WAS ABLE TO BRING HIS PRESUMED-DEAD SISTER SHURI BACK FROM **THE DJALIA**, A PLACE WHERE THE PAST, PRESENT, AND FUTURE OF WAKANDAN HISTORY EXIST ALL AT ONCE.

BUT **SHURI** RETURNED CHANGED, IMBUED WITH SUPERNATURAL POWERS THAT STILL REMAIN A MYSTERY. SHE COMES HOME TO FIND HER COUNTRYMEN RESTLESS: THE TEACHINGS OF THE PHILOSOPHY PROFESSOR **CHANGAMIRE** HAVE BECOME THE IDEALOGIC WAR DRUM FOR THE REBEL LEADER **TETU** AS HE ATTEMPTS TO INSTIGATE A FULL-BLOWN COUP USING TERRORISM. ONE SUCH TERRORIST BOMBING LED TO THE GRAVE INJURY OF QUEEN-MOTHER **RAMONDA**...

MEANWHILE, THE ROGUE **DORA MILAJE**, LED BY **THE MIDNIGHT ANGELS**—AYO AND ANEKA—HAVE TAKEN OVER THE JABARI-LANDS IN NORTHERN WAKANDA, SEVERING THEIR TIES TO THE ROYAL GOVERNMENT AND REDEDICATING THEMSELVES TO THE SERVICE OF WAKANDA.

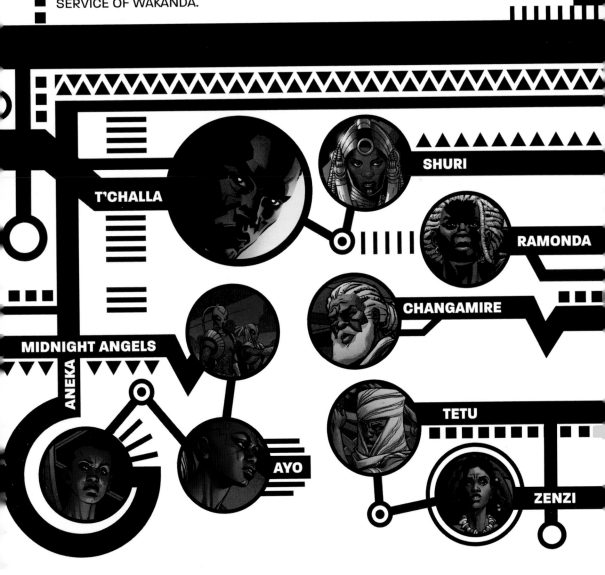

T'CHALLA

SHURI

RAMONDA

CHANGAMIRE

MIDNIGHT ANGELS

ANEKA

AYO

TETU

ZENZI

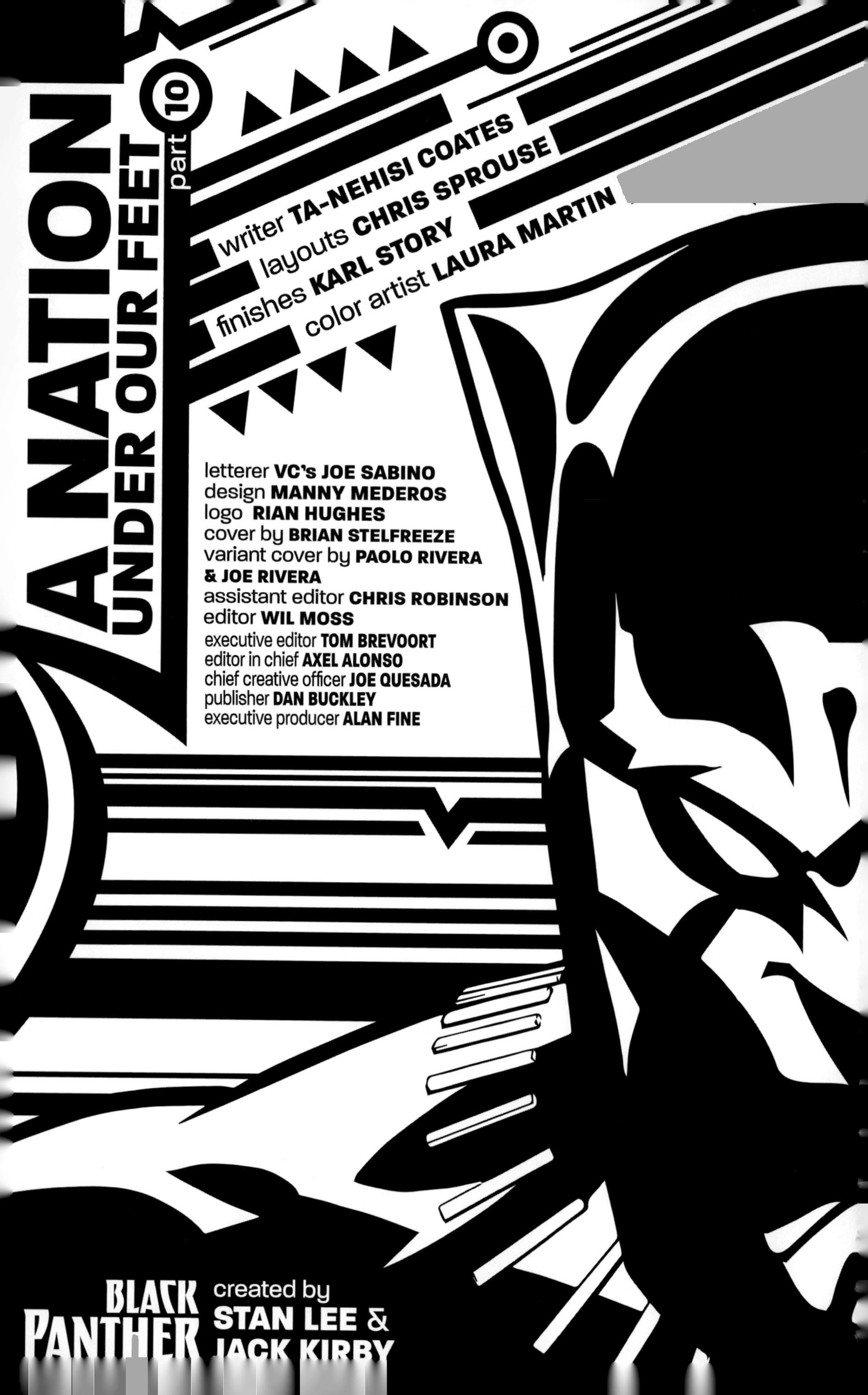

A NATION UNDER OUR FEET part 10

writer **TA-NEHISI COATES**
layouts **CHRIS SPROUSE**
finishes **KARL STORY**
color artist **LAURA MARTIN**

letterer **VC's JOE SABINO**
design **MANNY MEDEROS**
logo **RIAN HUGHES**
cover by **BRIAN STELFREEZE**
variant cover by **PAOLO RIVERA & JOE RIVERA**
assistant editor **CHRIS ROBINSON**
editor **WIL MOSS**
executive editor **TOM BREVOORT**
editor in chief **AXEL ALONSO**
chief creative officer **JOE QUESADA**
publisher **DAN BUCKLEY**
executive producer **ALAN FINE**

BLACK PANTHER created by **STAN LEE & JACK KIRBY**

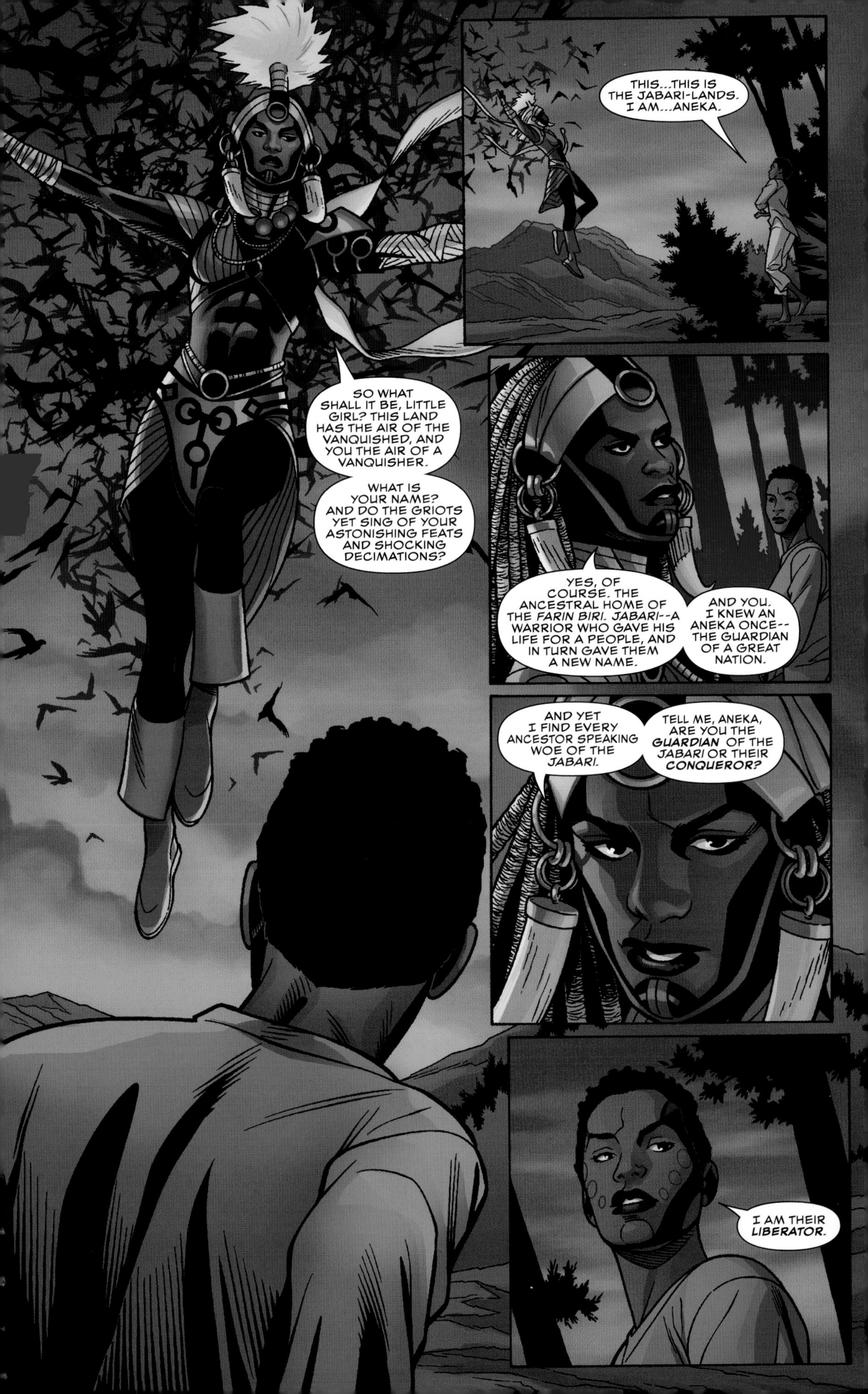
THIS...THIS IS THE JABARI-LANDS. I AM...ANEKA.
SO WHAT SHALL IT BE, LITTLE GIRL? THIS LAND HAS THE AIR OF THE VANQUISHED, AND YOU THE AIR OF A VANQUISHER.
WHAT IS YOUR NAME? AND DO THE GRIOTS YET SING OF YOUR ASTONISHING FEATS AND SHOCKING DECIMATIONS?
YES, OF COURSE. THE ANCESTRAL HOME OF THE *FARIN BIRI. JABARI*--A WARRIOR WHO GAVE HIS LIFE FOR A PEOPLE, AND IN TURN GAVE THEM A NEW NAME.
AND YOU. I KNEW AN ANEKA ONCE--THE GUARDIAN OF A GREAT NATION.
AND YET I FIND EVERY ANCESTOR SPEAKING WOE OF THE *JABARI*.
TELL ME, ANEKA, ARE YOU THE ***GUARDIAN*** OF THE *JABARI* OR THEIR ***CONQUEROR?***
I AM THEIR ***LIBERATOR***.

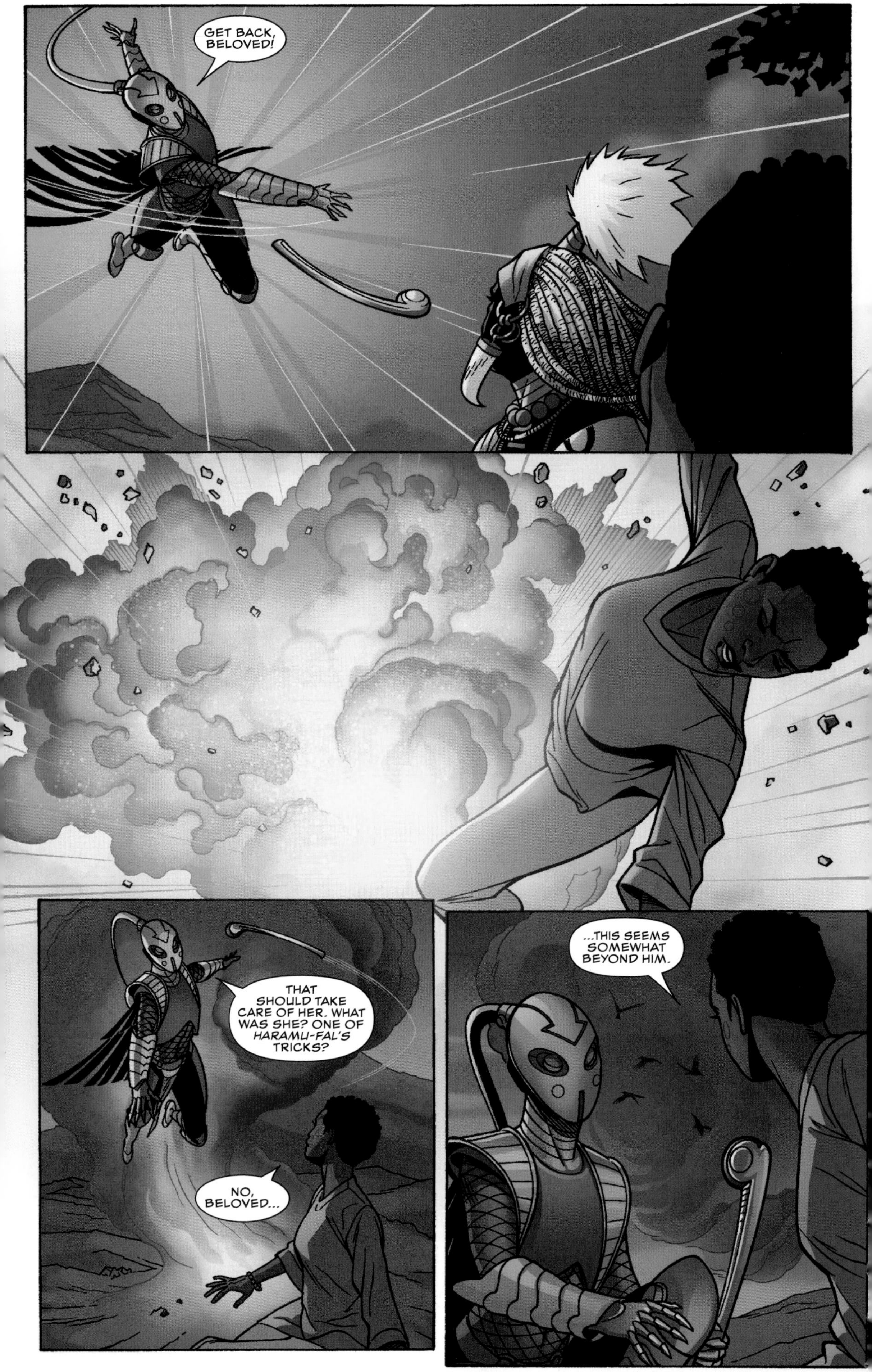
GET BACK, BELOVED!
THAT SHOULD TAKE CARE OF HER. WHAT WAS SHE? ONE OF HARAMU-FAL'S TRICKS?
NO, BELOVED...
...THIS SEEMS SOMEWHAT BEYOND HIM.

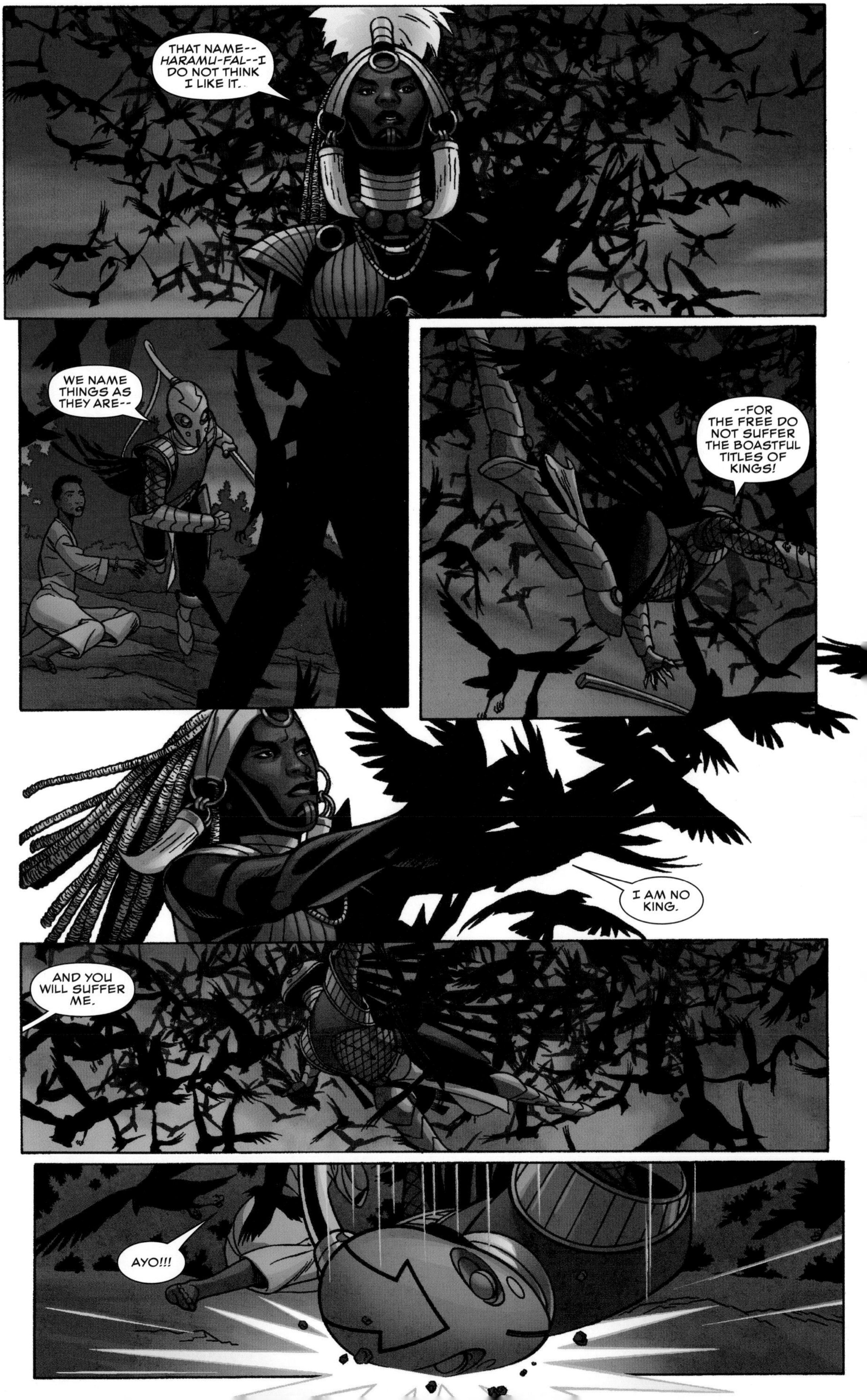
THAT NAME-- HARAMU-FAL--I DO NOT THINK I LIKE IT.
WE NAME THINGS AS THEY ARE--
--FOR THE FREE DO NOT SUFFER THE BOASTFUL TITLES OF KINGS!
I AM NO KING.
AND YOU WILL SUFFER ME.
AYO!!!

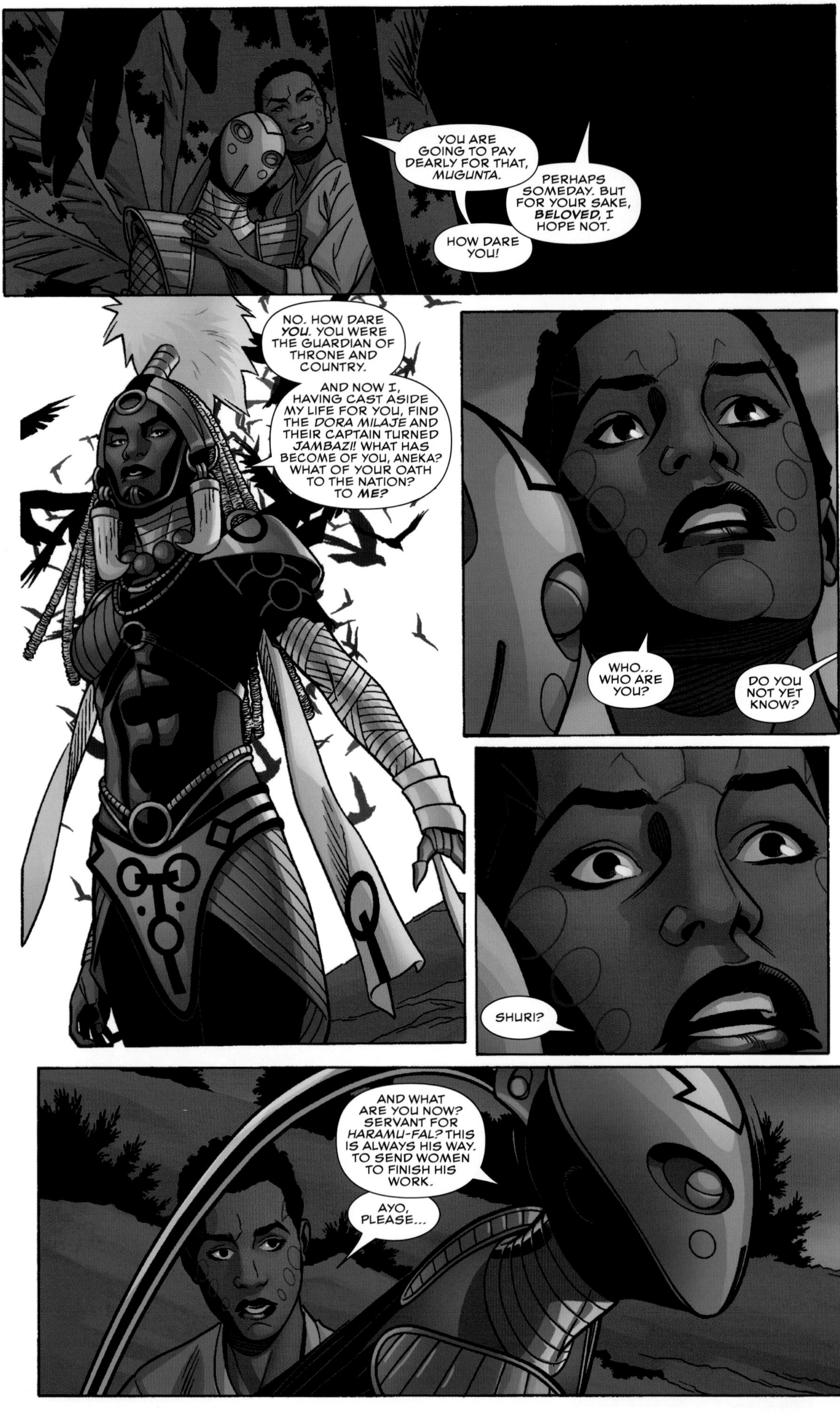
YOU ARE GOING TO PAY DEARLY FOR THAT, MUGUNTA.
HOW DARE YOU!
PERHAPS SOMEDAY. BUT FOR YOUR SAKE, BELOVED, I HOPE NOT.
NO. HOW DARE YOU. YOU WERE THE GUARDIAN OF THRONE AND COUNTRY.
AND NOW I, HAVING CAST ASIDE MY LIFE FOR YOU, FIND THE DORA MILAJE AND THEIR CAPTAIN TURNED JAMBAZI! WHAT HAS BECOME OF YOU, ANEKA? WHAT OF YOUR OATH TO THE NATION? TO ME?
WHO... WHO ARE YOU?
DO YOU NOT YET KNOW?
SHURI?
AND WHAT ARE YOU NOW? SERVANT FOR HARAMU-FAL? THIS IS ALWAYS HIS WAY. TO SEND WOMEN TO FINISH HIS WORK.
AYO, PLEASE...

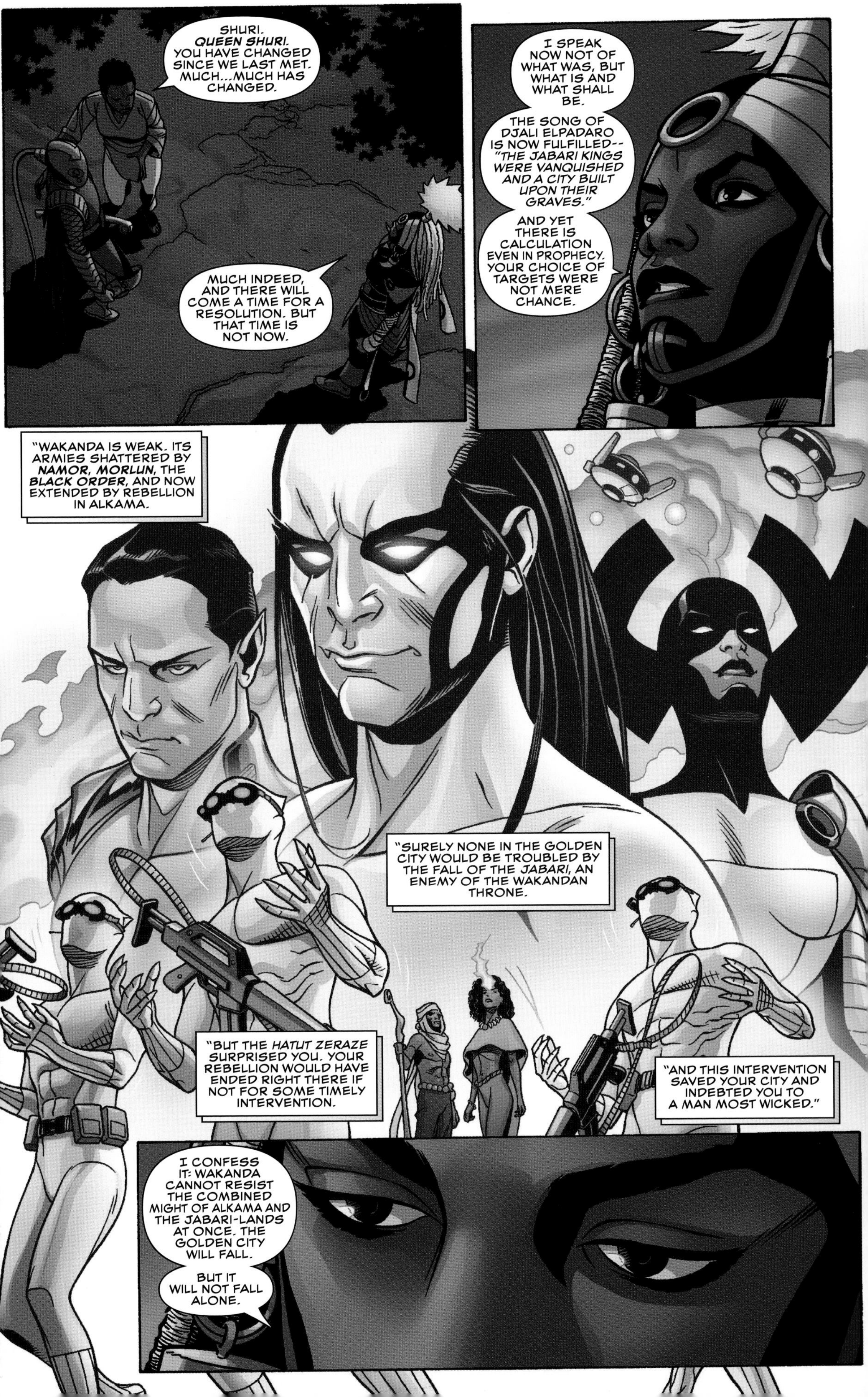
SHURI. QUEEN SHURI. YOU HAVE CHANGED SINCE WE LAST MET. MUCH... MUCH HAS CHANGED.
MUCH INDEED, AND THERE WILL COME A TIME FOR A RESOLUTION. BUT THAT TIME IS NOT NOW.
I SPEAK NOW NOT OF WHAT WAS, BUT WHAT IS AND WHAT SHALL BE.
THE SONG OF DJALI ELPADARO IS NOW FULFILLED-- "THE JABARI KINGS WERE VANQUISHED AND A CITY BUILT UPON THEIR GRAVES."
AND YET THERE IS CALCULATION EVEN IN PROPHECY. YOUR CHOICE OF TARGETS WERE NOT MERE CHANCE.
"WAKANDA IS WEAK. ITS ARMIES SHATTERED BY NAMOR, MORLUN, THE BLACK ORDER, AND NOW EXTENDED BY REBELLION IN ALKAMA.
"SURELY NONE IN THE GOLDEN CITY WOULD BE TROUBLED BY THE FALL OF THE JABARI, AN ENEMY OF THE WAKANDAN THRONE.
"BUT THE HATUT ZERAZE SURPRISED YOU. YOUR REBELLION WOULD HAVE ENDED RIGHT THERE IF NOT FOR SOME TIMELY INTERVENTION.
"AND THIS INTERVENTION SAVED YOUR CITY AND INDEBTED YOU TO A MAN MOST WICKED."
I CONFESS IT: WAKANDA CANNOT RESIST THE COMBINED MIGHT OF ALKAMA AND THE JABARI-LANDS AT ONCE. THE GOLDEN CITY WILL FALL.
BUT IT WILL NOT FALL ALONE.

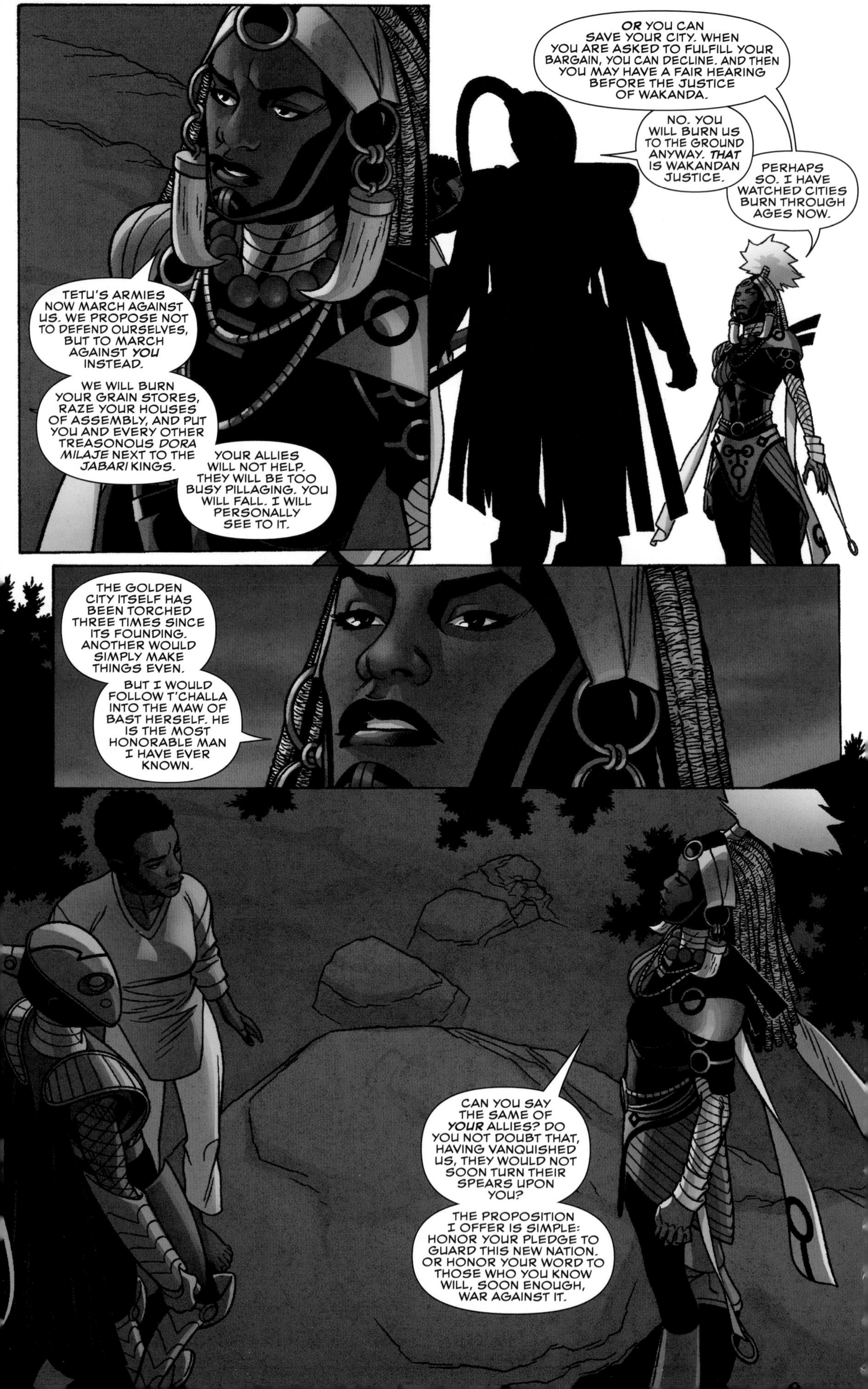
TETU'S ARMIES NOW MARCH AGAINST US. WE PROPOSE NOT TO DEFEND OURSELVES, BUT TO MARCH AGAINST *YOU* INSTEAD.
WE WILL BURN YOUR GRAIN STORES, RAZE YOUR HOUSES OF ASSEMBLY, AND PUT YOU AND EVERY OTHER TREASONOUS *DORA MILAJE* NEXT TO THE *JABARI* KINGS.
YOUR ALLIES WILL NOT HELP. THEY WILL BE TOO BUSY PILLAGING. YOU WILL FALL. I WILL PERSONALLY SEE TO IT.
OR YOU CAN SAVE YOUR CITY. WHEN YOU ARE ASKED TO FULFILL YOUR BARGAIN, YOU CAN DECLINE. AND THEN YOU MAY HAVE A FAIR HEARING BEFORE THE JUSTICE OF WAKANDA.
NO. YOU WILL BURN US TO THE GROUND ANYWAY. ***THAT*** IS WAKANDAN JUSTICE.
PERHAPS SO. I HAVE WATCHED CITIES BURN THROUGH AGES NOW.
THE GOLDEN CITY ITSELF HAS BEEN TORCHED THREE TIMES SINCE ITS FOUNDING. ANOTHER WOULD SIMPLY MAKE THINGS EVEN.
BUT I WOULD FOLLOW T'CHALLA INTO THE MAW OF BAST HERSELF. HE IS THE MOST HONORABLE MAN I HAVE EVER KNOWN.
CAN YOU SAY THE SAME OF ***YOUR*** ALLIES? DO YOU NOT DOUBT THAT, HAVING VANQUISHED US, THEY WOULD NOT SOON TURN THEIR SPEARS UPON YOU?
THE PROPOSITION I OFFER IS SIMPLE: HONOR YOUR PLEDGE TO GUARD THIS NEW NATION. OR HONOR YOUR WORD TO THOSE WHO YOU KNOW WILL, SOON ENOUGH, WAR AGAINST IT.

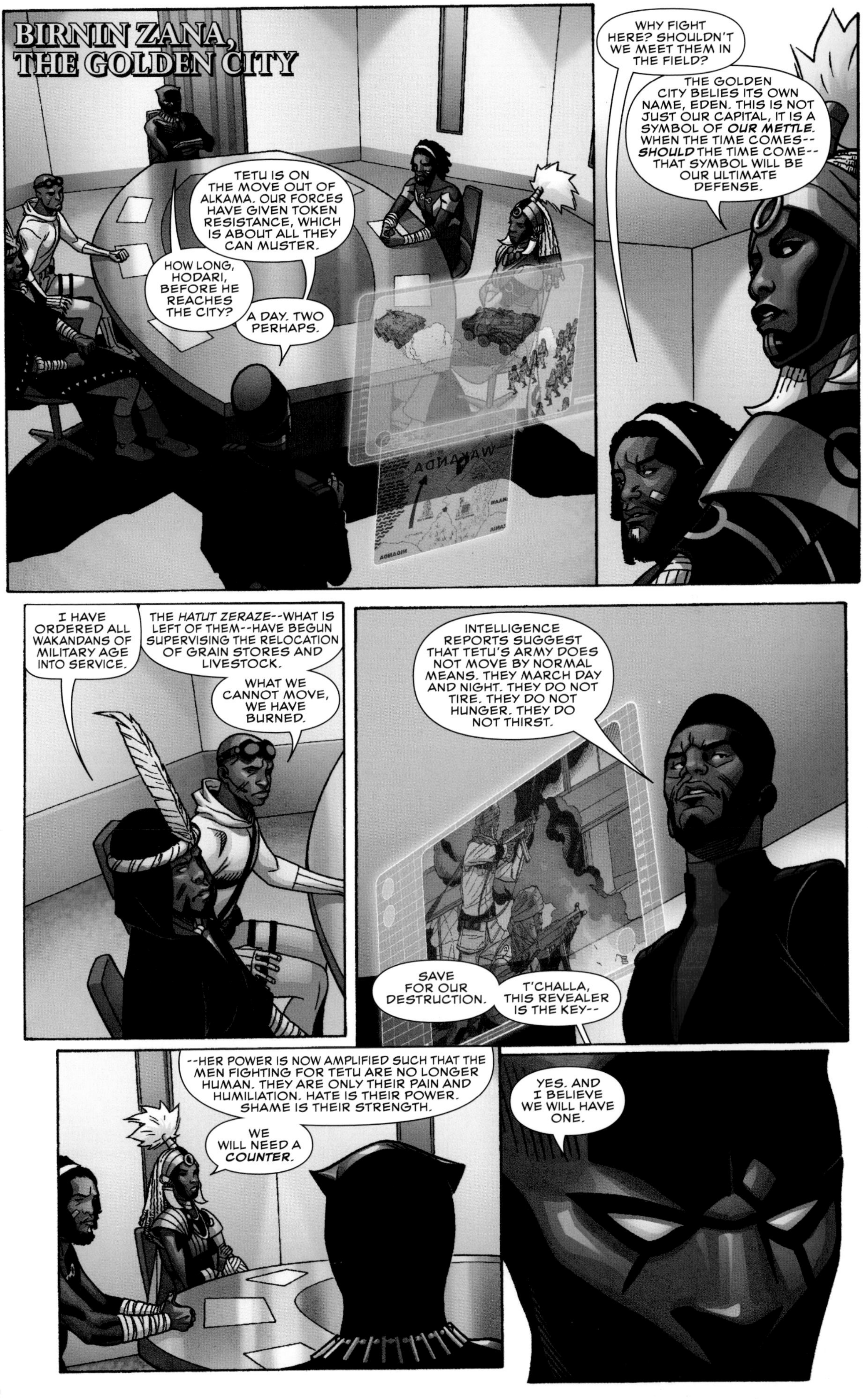
BIRNIN ZANA, THE GOLDEN CITY
TETU IS ON THE MOVE OUT OF ALKAMA. OUR FORCES HAVE GIVEN TOKEN RESISTANCE, WHICH IS ABOUT ALL THEY CAN MUSTER.
HOW LONG, HODARI, BEFORE HE REACHES THE CITY?
A DAY. TWO PERHAPS.
WHY FIGHT HERE? SHOULDN'T WE MEET THEM IN THE FIELD?
THE GOLDEN CITY BELIES ITS OWN NAME, EDEN. THIS IS NOT JUST OUR CAPITAL, IT IS A SYMBOL OF *OUR METTLE.* WHEN THE TIME COMES-- *SHOULD* THE TIME COME-- THAT SYMBOL WILL BE OUR ULTIMATE DEFENSE.
I HAVE ORDERED ALL WAKANDANS OF MILITARY AGE INTO SERVICE.
THE *HATUT ZERAZE*--WHAT IS LEFT OF THEM--HAVE BEGUN SUPERVISING THE RELOCATION OF GRAIN STORES AND LIVESTOCK.
WHAT WE CANNOT MOVE, WE HAVE BURNED.
INTELLIGENCE REPORTS SUGGEST THAT TETU'S ARMY DOES NOT MOVE BY NORMAL MEANS. THEY MARCH DAY AND NIGHT. THEY DO NOT TIRE. THEY DO NOT HUNGER. THEY DO NOT THIRST.
SAVE FOR OUR DESTRUCTION.
T'CHALLA, THIS REVEALER IS THE KEY--
--HER POWER IS NOW AMPLIFIED SUCH THAT THE MEN FIGHTING FOR TETU ARE NO LONGER HUMAN. THEY ARE ONLY THEIR PAIN AND HUMILIATION. HATE IS THEIR POWER. SHAME IS THEIR STRENGTH.
WE WILL NEED A *COUNTER.*
YES. AND I BELIEVE WE WILL HAVE ONE.

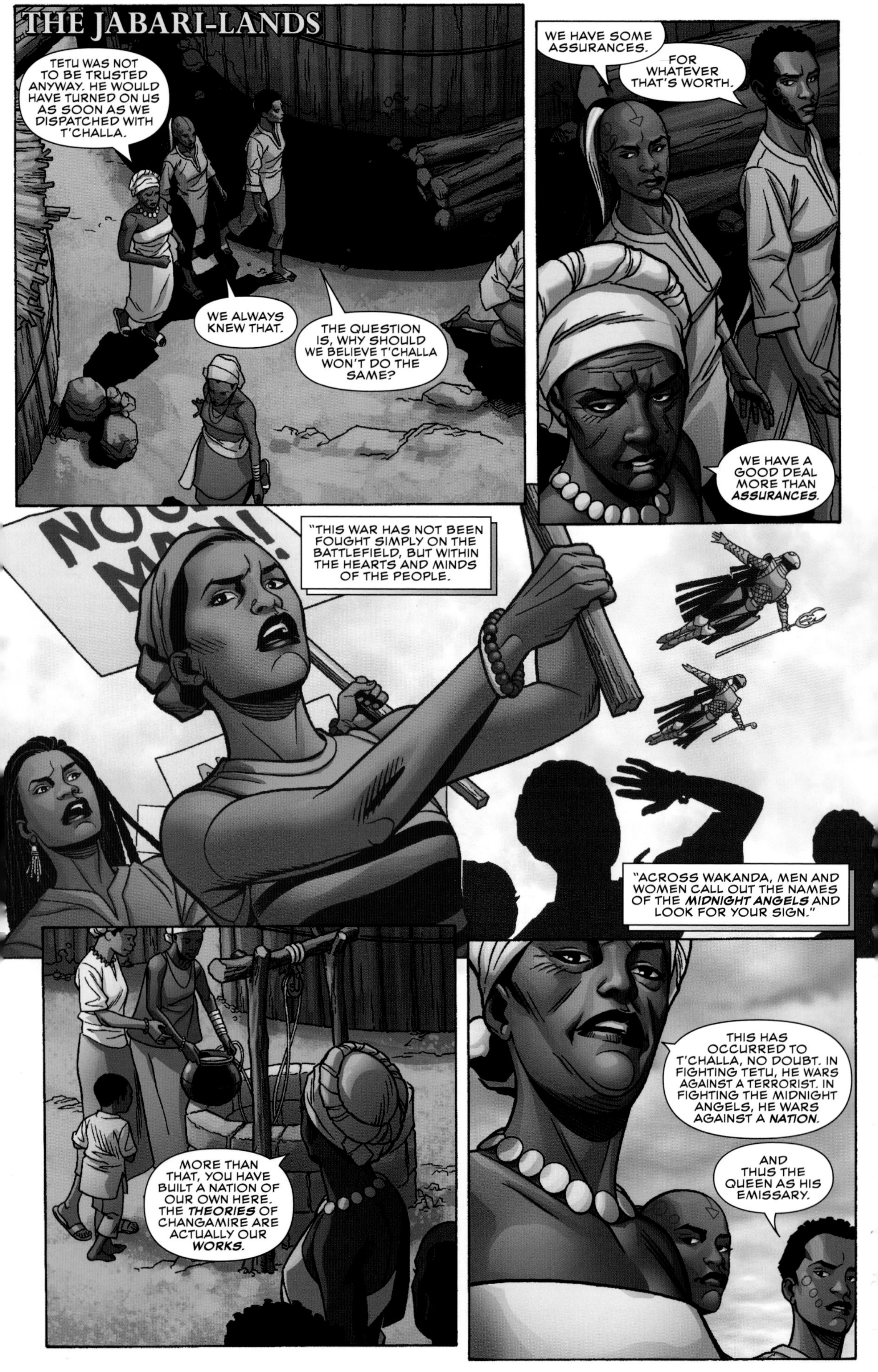
THE JABARI-LANDS
TETU WAS NOT TO BE TRUSTED ANYWAY. HE WOULD HAVE TURNED ON US AS SOON AS WE DISPATCHED WITH T'CHALLA.
WE ALWAYS KNEW THAT.
THE QUESTION IS, WHY SHOULD WE BELIEVE T'CHALLA WON'T DO THE SAME?
WE HAVE SOME ASSURANCES.
—FOR WHATEVER THAT'S WORTH.
WE HAVE A GOOD DEAL MORE THAN *ASSURANCES*.
"THIS WAR HAS NOT BEEN FOUGHT SIMPLY ON THE BATTLEFIELD, BUT WITHIN THE HEARTS AND MINDS OF THE PEOPLE.
"ACROSS WAKANDA, MEN AND WOMEN CALL OUT THE NAMES OF THE *MIDNIGHT ANGELS* AND LOOK FOR YOUR SIGN."
MORE THAN THAT, YOU HAVE BUILT A NATION OF OUR OWN HERE. THE *THEORIES* OF CHANGAMIRE ARE ACTUALLY OUR *WORKS*.
THIS HAS OCCURRED TO T'CHALLA, NO DOUBT. IN FIGHTING TETU, HE WARS AGAINST A TERRORIST. IN FIGHTING THE MIDNIGHT ANGELS, HE WARS AGAINST A *NATION*.
AND THUS THE QUEEN AS HIS EMISSARY.

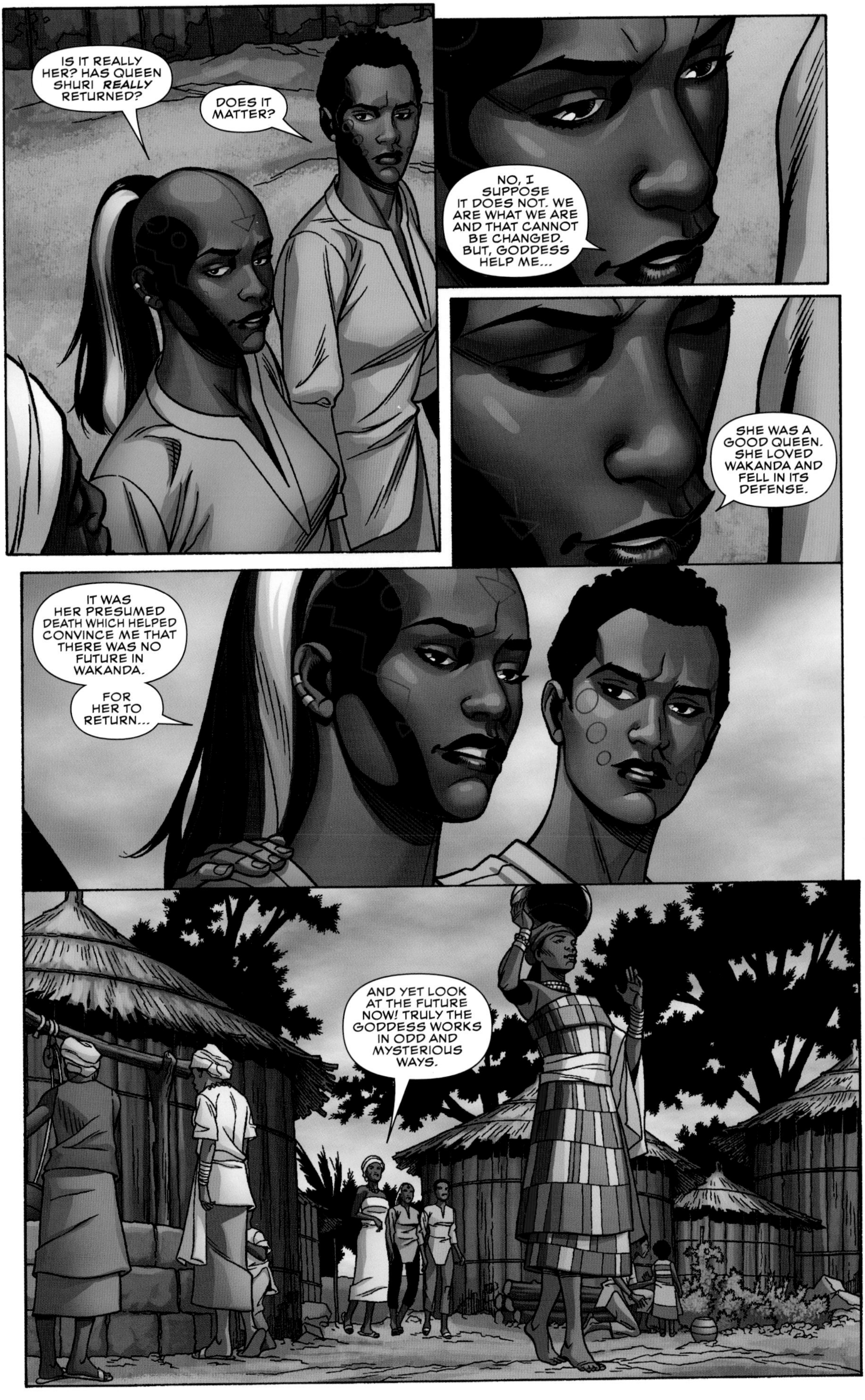
IS IT REALLY HER? HAS QUEEN SHURI *REALLY* RETURNED?
DOES IT MATTER?
NO, I SUPPOSE IT DOES NOT. WE ARE WHAT WE ARE AND THAT CANNOT BE CHANGED. BUT, GODDESS HELP ME...
SHE WAS A GOOD QUEEN. SHE LOVED WAKANDA AND FELL IN ITS DEFENSE.
IT WAS HER PRESUMED DEATH WHICH HELPED CONVINCE ME THAT THERE WAS NO FUTURE IN WAKANDA.
FOR HER TO RETURN...
AND YET LOOK AT THE FUTURE NOW! TRULY THE GODDESS WORKS IN ODD AND MYSTERIOUS WAYS.

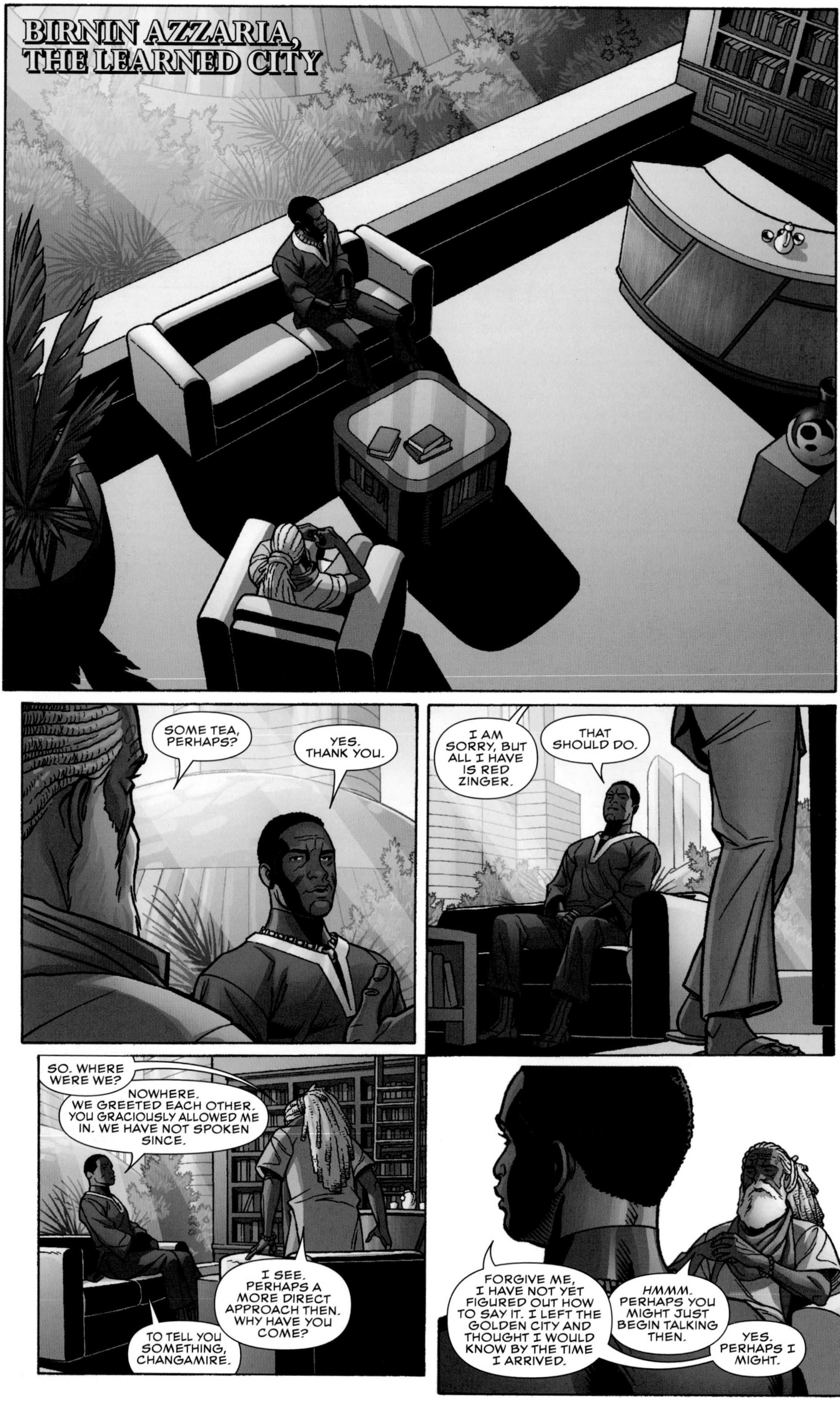
BIRNIN AZZARIA, THE LEARNED CITY
SOME TEA, PERHAPS?
YES. THANK YOU.
I AM SORRY, BUT ALL I HAVE IS RED ZINGER.
THAT SHOULD DO.
SO. WHERE WERE WE?
NOWHERE. WE GREETED EACH OTHER. YOU GRACIOUSLY ALLOWED ME IN. WE HAVE NOT SPOKEN SINCE.
I SEE. PERHAPS A MORE DIRECT APPROACH THEN. WHY HAVE YOU COME?
TO TELL YOU SOMETHING, CHANGAMIRE.
FORGIVE ME, I HAVE NOT YET FIGURED OUT HOW TO SAY IT. I LEFT THE GOLDEN CITY AND THOUGHT I WOULD KNOW BY THE TIME I ARRIVED.
HMMM. PERHAPS YOU MIGHT JUST BEGIN TALKING THEN.
YES. PERHAPS I MIGHT.

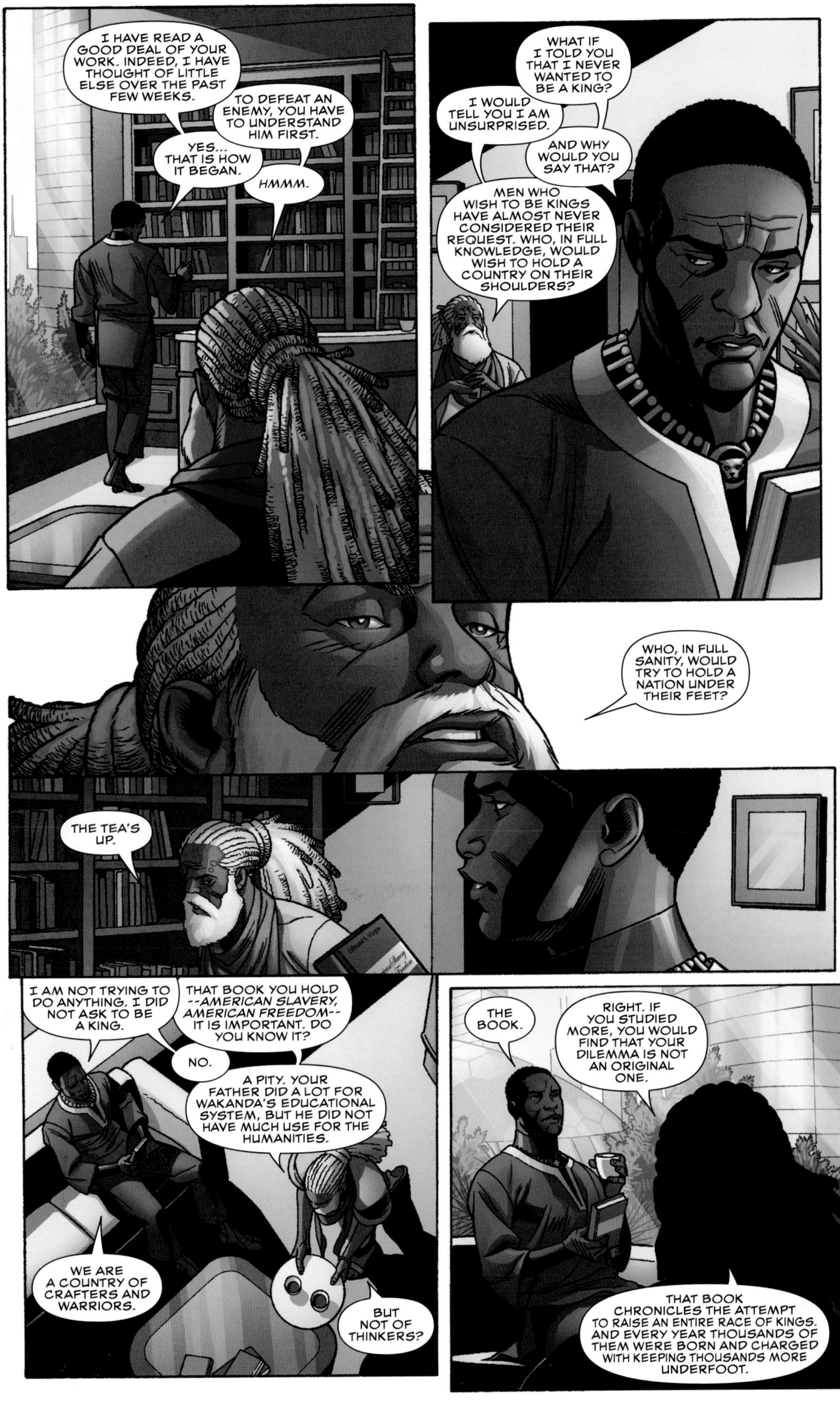
I HAVE READ A GOOD DEAL OF YOUR WORK. INDEED, I HAVE THOUGHT OF LITTLE ELSE OVER THE PAST FEW WEEKS.
TO DEFEAT AN ENEMY, YOU HAVE TO UNDERSTAND HIM FIRST.
YES... THAT IS HOW IT BEGAN.
HMMM.
WHAT IF I TOLD YOU THAT I NEVER WANTED TO BE A KING?
I WOULD TELL YOU I AM UNSURPRISED.
AND WHY WOULD YOU SAY THAT?
MEN WHO WISH TO BE KINGS HAVE ALMOST NEVER CONSIDERED THEIR REQUEST. WHO, IN FULL KNOWLEDGE, WOULD WISH TO HOLD A COUNTRY ON THEIR SHOULDERS?
WHO, IN FULL SANITY, WOULD TRY TO HOLD A NATION UNDER THEIR FEET?
THE TEA'S UP.
I AM NOT TRYING TO DO ANYTHING. I DID NOT ASK TO BE A KING.
THAT BOOK YOU HOLD --AMERICAN SLAVERY, AMERICAN FREEDOM-- IT IS IMPORTANT. DO YOU KNOW IT?
NO.
A PITY. YOUR FATHER DID A LOT FOR WAKANDA'S EDUCATIONAL SYSTEM, BUT HE DID NOT HAVE MUCH USE FOR THE HUMANITIES.
WE ARE A COUNTRY OF CRAFTERS AND WARRIORS.
BUT NOT OF THINKERS?
THE BOOK.
RIGHT. IF YOU STUDIED MORE, YOU WOULD FIND THAT YOUR DILEMMA IS NOT AN ORIGINAL ONE.
THAT BOOK CHRONICLES THE ATTEMPT TO RAISE AN ENTIRE RACE OF KINGS. AND EVERY YEAR THOUSANDS OF THEM WERE BORN AND CHARGED WITH KEEPING THOUSANDS MORE UNDERFOOT.

CAN YOU IMAGINE IT? WHOLE GENERATIONS BROUGHT UP WITH THE DAILY WEIGHT OF TURNING THEIR FELLOW MAN INTO SLAVES.

IT DROVE THEM MAD, YOU UNDERSTAND. THEY SLAUGHTERED EACH OTHER BY THE SCORE. WHOLE GENERATIONS TURNED TO DUST. ALL FOR THE RIGHT TO LIVE AS KINGS.

WHAT HAPPENED TO THE SLAVES?

THE SLAVES? IT WAS THE SLAVES WHO STARTED THE WAR. THEIR COUNTRY MERELY JOINED IN.

BUT THE SLAVES ARE FREE NOW, ARE THEY NOT?

IT IS TOO SOON TO TELL, MY KING.

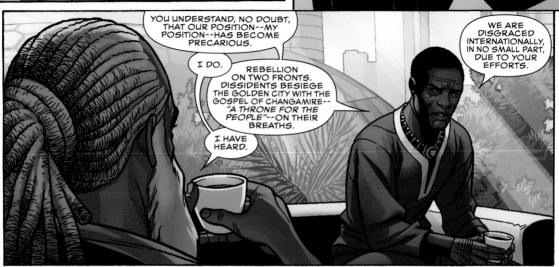

YOU UNDERSTAND, NO DOUBT, THAT OUR POSITION--MY POSITION--HAS BECOME PRECARIOUS.

I DO.

REBELLION ON TWO FRONTS. DISSIDENTS BESIEGE THE GOLDEN CITY WITH THE GOSPEL OF CHANGAMIRE-- "A THRONE FOR THE PEOPLE"--ON THEIR BREATHS.

I HAVE HEARD.

WE ARE DISGRACED INTERNATIONALLY, IN NO SMALL PART, DUE TO YOUR EFFORTS.

HAVE YOU COME TO ARREST ME?

NO. I THINK NOT. ON THE CONTRARY, I HAVE COME TO ASK FOR YOUR HELP.

AND HOW COULD I HELP?

YOU CAN TELL ME WHAT I SHOULD DO.

FRANKLY, I HAVE NO IDEA.

YES. I KNOW.

YOU ARE A VOYAGER WITHOUT A SHIP. DREAMING OF DISTANT LANDS BUT WITH NO MEANS TO REACH THEM.

AND YOU ARE AN INDUSTRIALIST BORN TO A THOUSAND SHIPS. MAROONED HERE WITH THE WEST AND THE REST OF US.

INDEED.

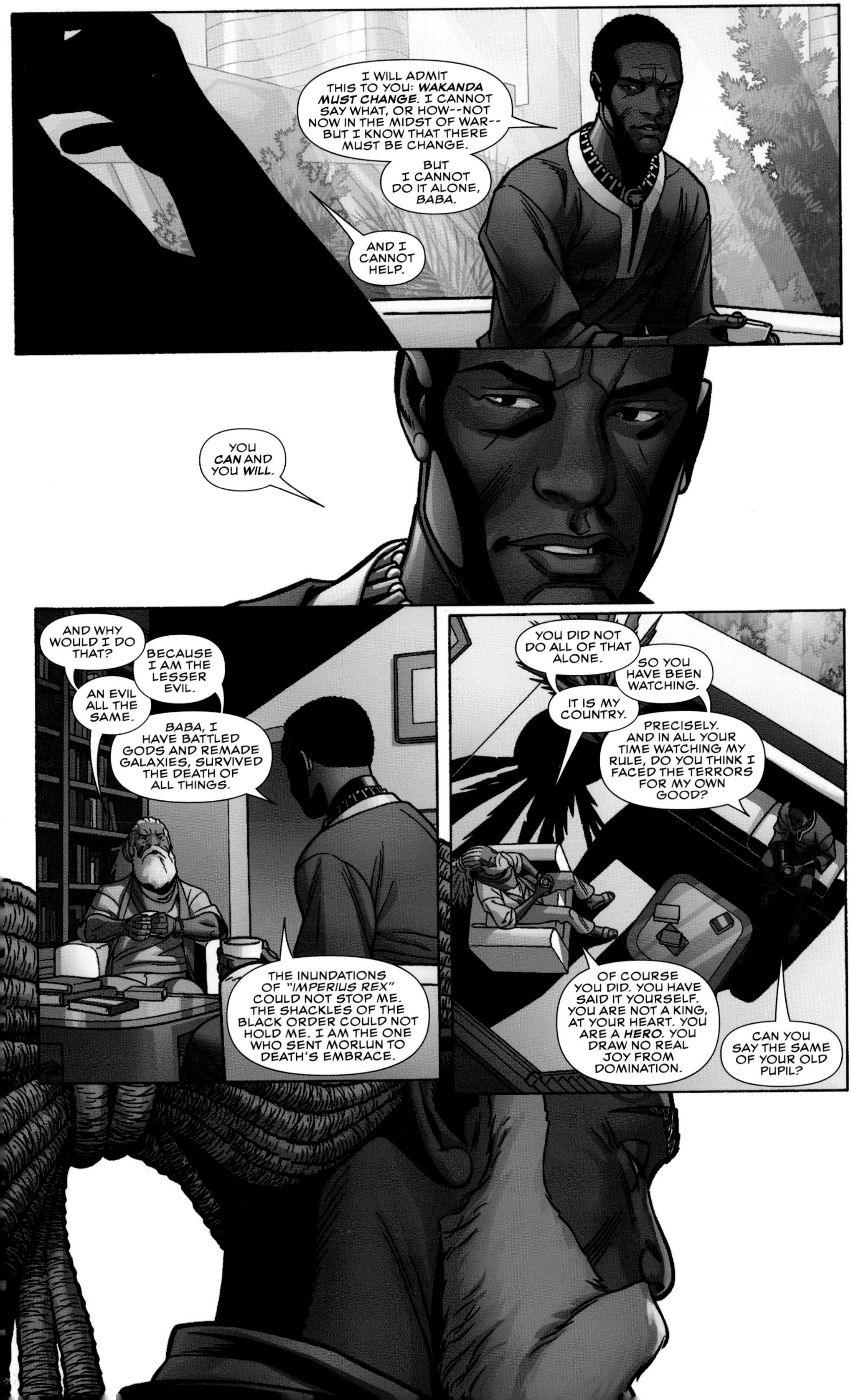
I WILL ADMIT THIS TO YOU: WAKANDA MUST CHANGE. I CANNOT SAY WHAT, OR HOW--NOT NOW IN THE MIDST OF WAR--BUT I KNOW THAT THERE MUST BE CHANGE.
BUT I CANNOT DO IT ALONE, BABA.
AND I CANNOT HELP.
YOU CAN AND YOU WILL.
AND WHY WOULD I DO THAT?
BECAUSE I AM THE LESSER EVIL.
AN EVIL ALL THE SAME.
BABA, I HAVE BATTLED GODS AND REMADE GALAXIES, SURVIVED THE DEATH OF ALL THINGS.
THE INUNDATIONS OF "IMPERIUS REX" COULD NOT STOP ME. THE SHACKLES OF THE BLACK ORDER COULD NOT HOLD ME. I AM THE ONE WHO SENT MORLUN TO DEATH'S EMBRACE.
YOU DID NOT DO ALL OF THAT ALONE.
SO YOU HAVE BEEN WATCHING.
IT IS MY COUNTRY.
PRECISELY. AND IN ALL YOUR TIME WATCHING MY RULE, DO YOU THINK I FACED THE TERRORS FOR MY OWN GOOD?
OF COURSE YOU DID. YOU HAVE SAID IT YOURSELF. YOU ARE NOT A KING, AT YOUR HEART. YOU ARE A HERO. YOU DRAW NO REAL JOY FROM DOMINATION.
CAN YOU SAY THE SAME OF YOUR OLD PUPIL?

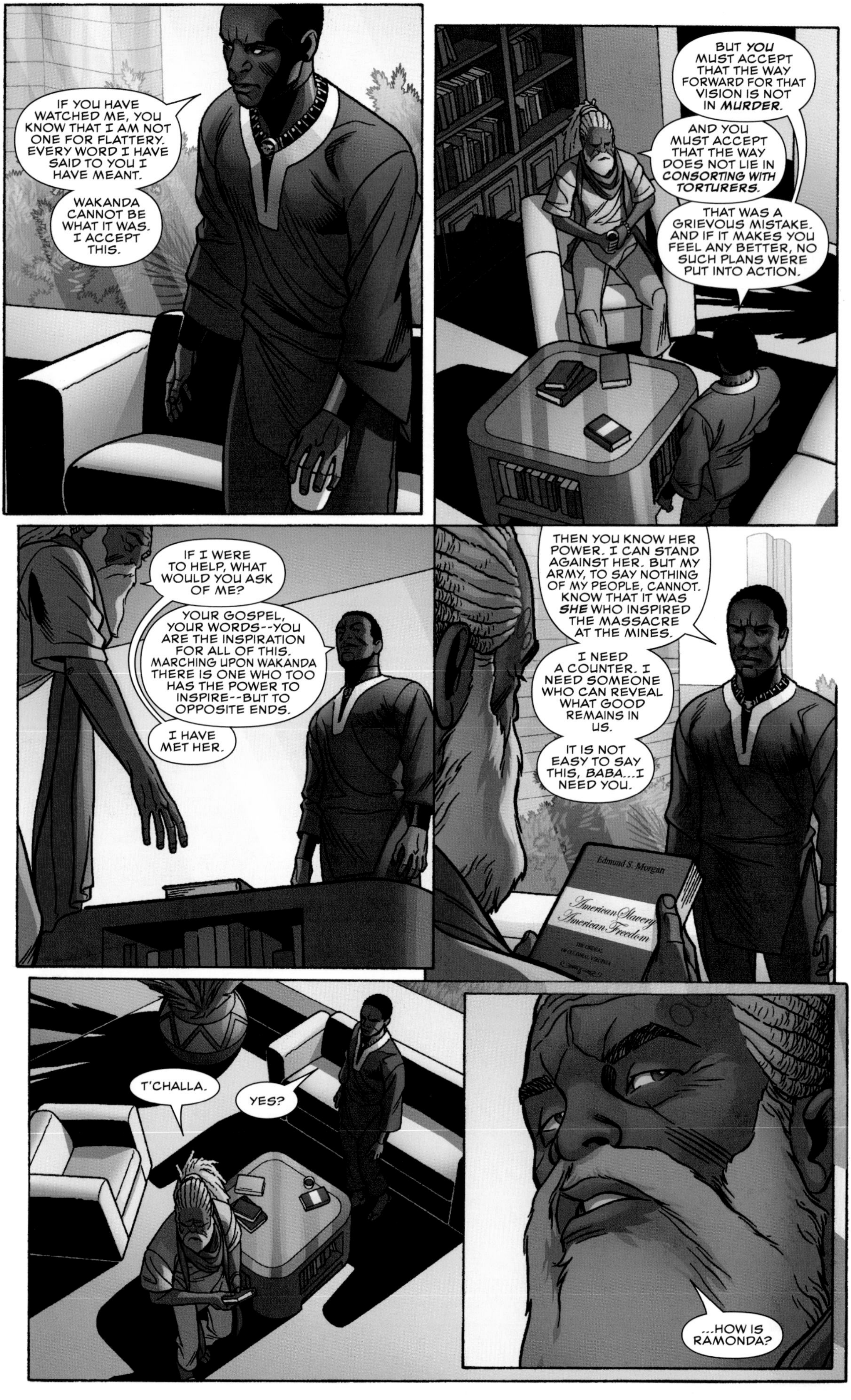
IF YOU HAVE WATCHED ME, YOU KNOW THAT I AM NOT ONE FOR FLATTERY. EVERY WORD I HAVE SAID TO YOU I HAVE MEANT.
WAKANDA CANNOT BE WHAT IT WAS. I ACCEPT THIS.
BUT YOU MUST ACCEPT THAT THE WAY FORWARD FOR THAT VISION IS NOT IN MURDER.
AND YOU MUST ACCEPT THAT THE WAY DOES NOT LIE IN CONSORTING WITH TORTURERS.
THAT WAS A GRIEVOUS MISTAKE. AND IF IT MAKES YOU FEEL ANY BETTER, NO SUCH PLANS WERE PUT INTO ACTION.
IF I WERE TO HELP, WHAT WOULD YOU ASK OF ME?
YOUR GOSPEL, YOUR WORDS--YOU ARE THE INSPIRATION FOR ALL OF THIS. MARCHING UPON WAKANDA THERE IS ONE WHO TOO HAS THE POWER TO INSPIRE--BUT TO OPPOSITE ENDS.
I HAVE MET HER.
THEN YOU KNOW HER POWER. I CAN STAND AGAINST HER. BUT MY ARMY, TO SAY NOTHING OF MY PEOPLE, CANNOT. KNOW THAT IT WAS SHE WHO INSPIRED THE MASSACRE AT THE MINES.
I NEED A COUNTER. I NEED SOMEONE WHO CAN REVEAL WHAT GOOD REMAINS IN US.
IT IS NOT EASY TO SAY THIS, BABA... I NEED YOU.
Edmund S. Morgan
American Slavery American Freedom
T'CHALLA.
YES?
...HOW IS RAMONDA?

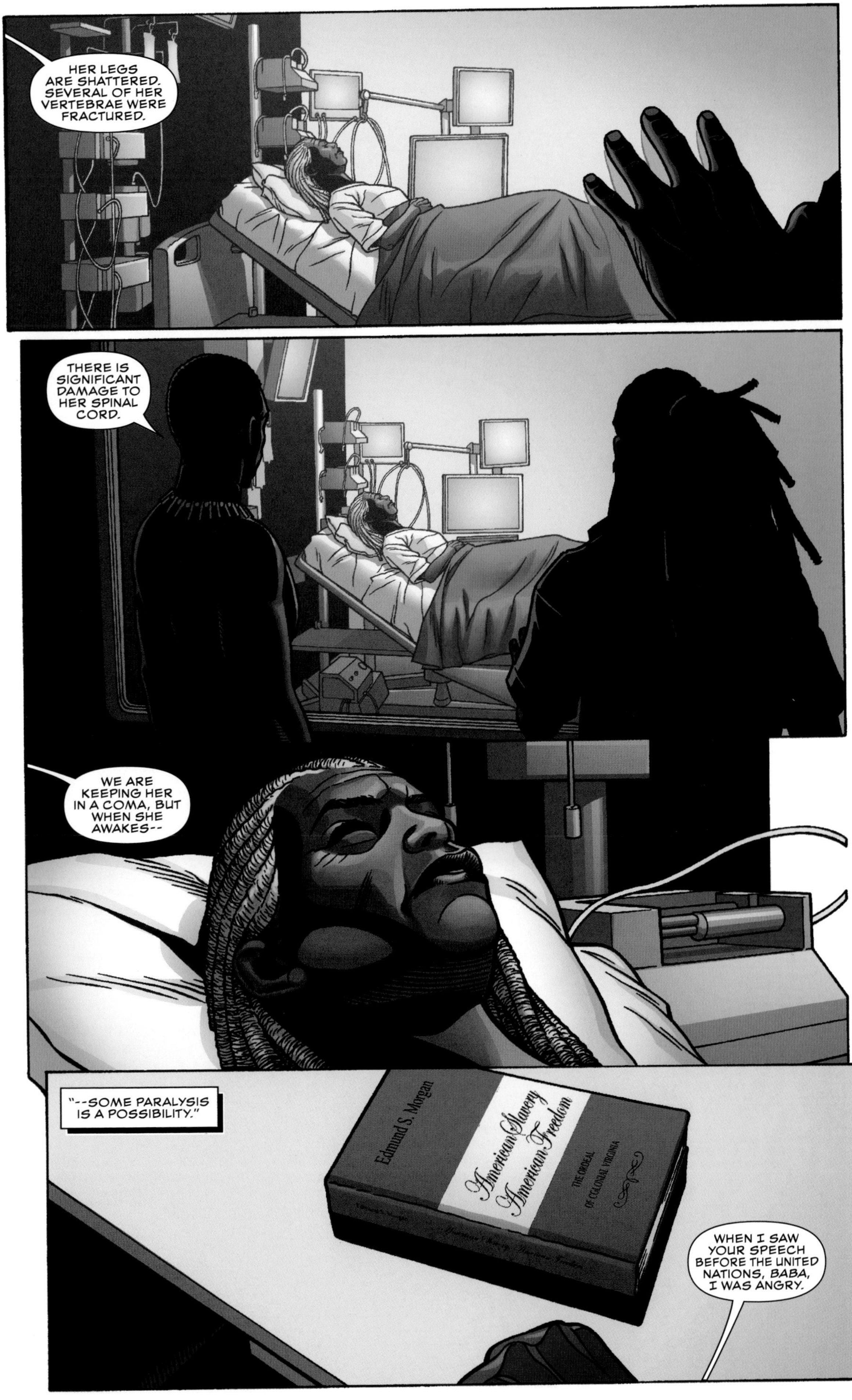
HER LEGS ARE SHATTERED. SEVERAL OF HER VERTEBRAE WERE FRACTURED.
THERE IS SIGNIFICANT DAMAGE TO HER SPINAL CORD.
WE ARE KEEPING HER IN A COMA, BUT WHEN SHE AWAKES--
"--SOME PARALYSIS IS A POSSIBILITY."
Edmund S. Morgan
American Slavery American Freedom
THE ORDEAL OF COLONIAL VIRGINIA
WHEN I SAW YOUR SPEECH BEFORE THE UNITED NATIONS, BABA, I WAS ANGRY.

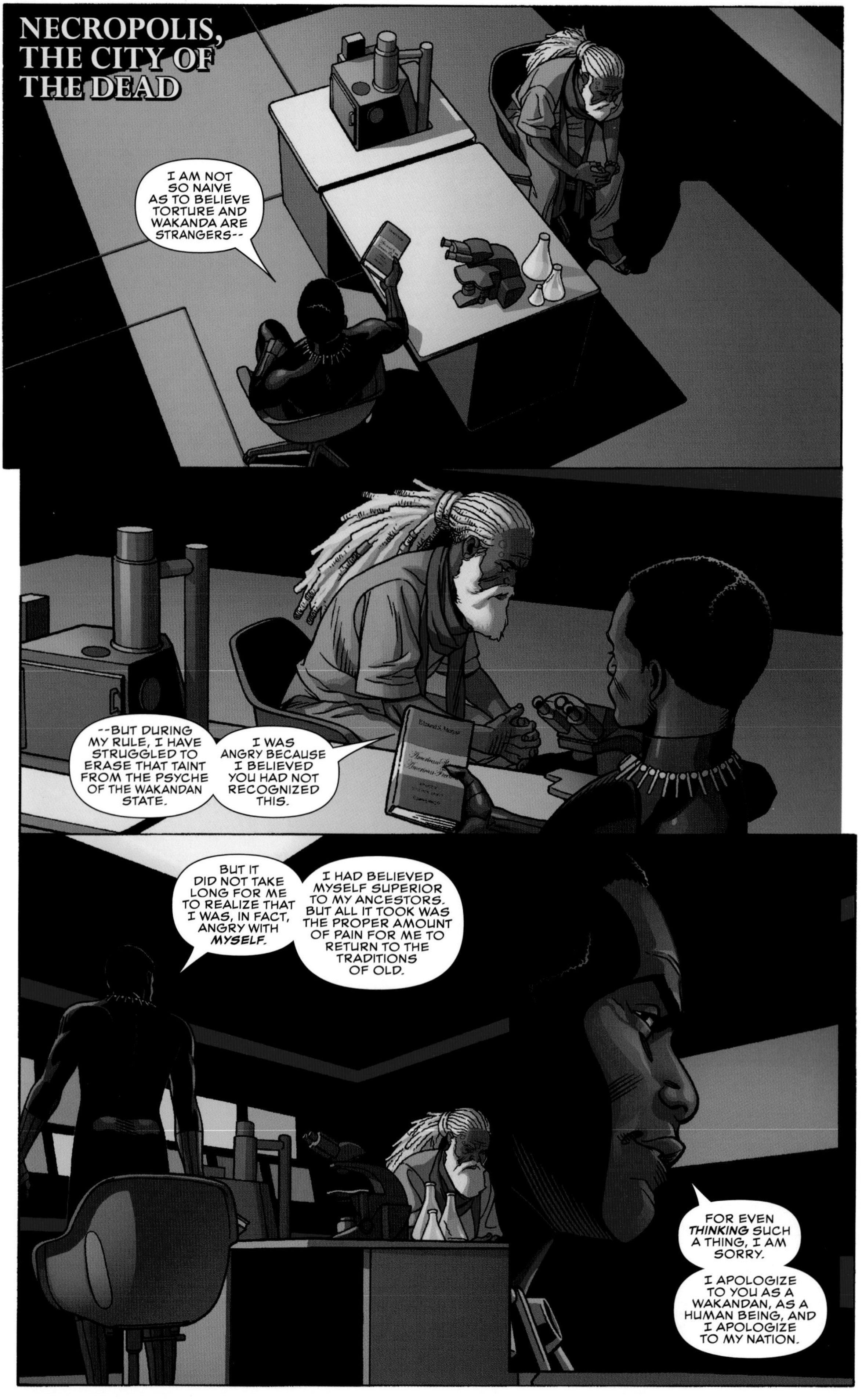
NECROPOLIS, THE CITY OF THE DEAD
I AM NOT SO NAIVE AS TO BELIEVE TORTURE AND WAKANDA ARE STRANGERS--
--BUT DURING MY RULE, I HAVE STRUGGLED TO ERASE THAT TAINT FROM THE PSYCHE OF THE WAKANDAN STATE.
I WAS ANGRY BECAUSE I BELIEVED YOU HAD NOT RECOGNIZED THIS.
BUT IT DID NOT TAKE LONG FOR ME TO REALIZE THAT I WAS, IN FACT, ANGRY WITH *MYSELF*.
I HAD BELIEVED MYSELF SUPERIOR TO MY ANCESTORS. BUT ALL IT TOOK WAS THE PROPER AMOUNT OF PAIN FOR ME TO RETURN TO THE TRADITIONS OF OLD.
FOR EVEN *THINKING* SUCH A THING, I AM SORRY.
I APOLOGIZE TO YOU AS A WAKANDAN, AS A HUMAN BEING, AND I APOLOGIZE TO MY NATION.

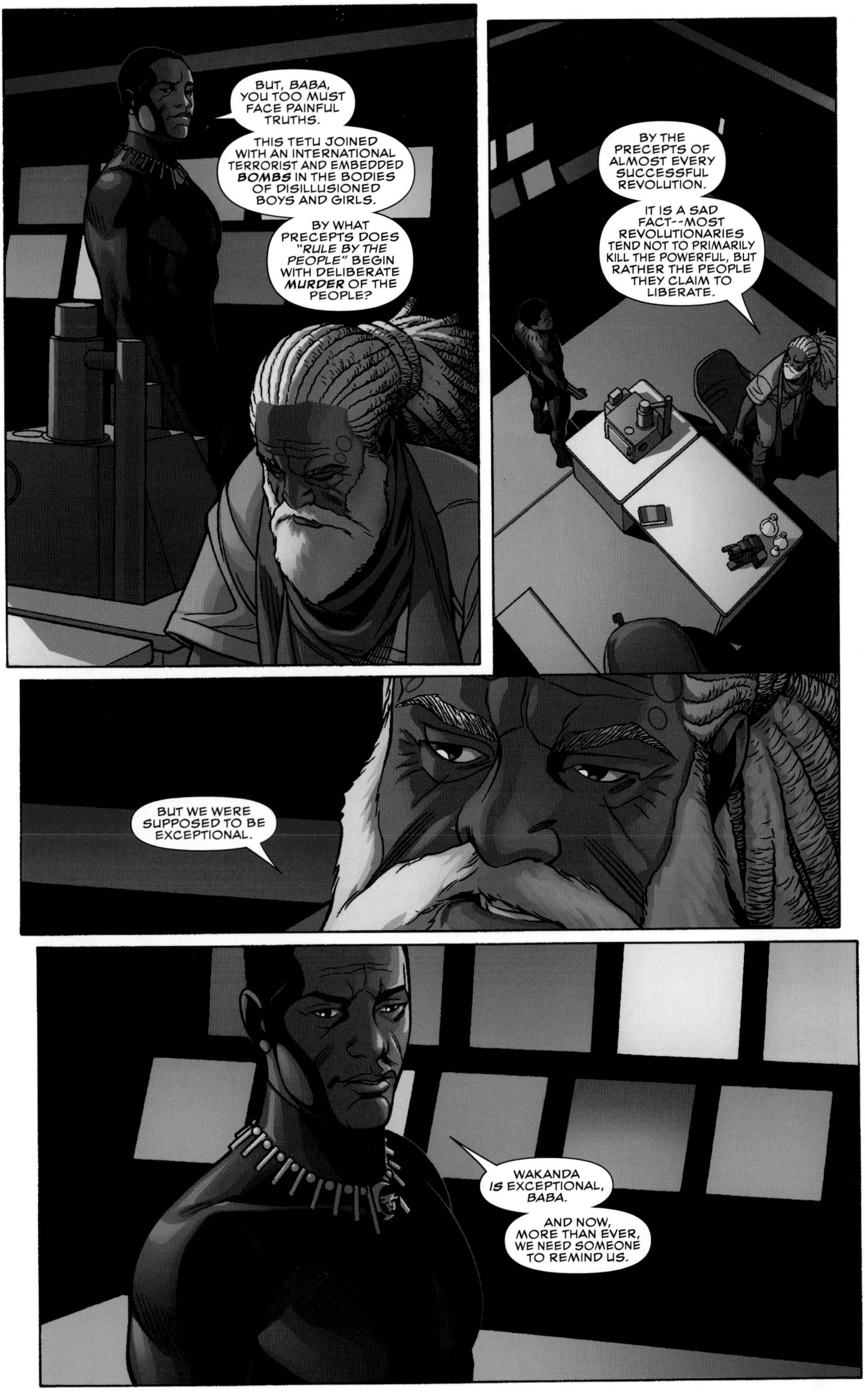
BUT, BABA, YOU TOO MUST FACE PAINFUL TRUTHS.
THIS TETU JOINED WITH AN INTERNATIONAL TERRORIST AND EMBEDDED BOMBS IN THE BODIES OF DISILLUSIONED BOYS AND GIRLS.
BY WHAT PRECEPTS DOES "RULE BY THE PEOPLE" BEGIN WITH DELIBERATE MURDER OF THE PEOPLE?
BY THE PRECEPTS OF ALMOST EVERY SUCCESSFUL REVOLUTION.
IT IS A SAD FACT--MOST REVOLUTIONARIES TEND NOT TO PRIMARILY KILL THE POWERFUL, BUT RATHER THE PEOPLE THEY CLAIM TO LIBERATE.
BUT WE WERE SUPPOSED TO BE EXCEPTIONAL.
WAKANDA IS EXCEPTIONAL, BABA.
AND NOW, MORE THAN EVER, WE NEED SOMEONE TO REMIND US.

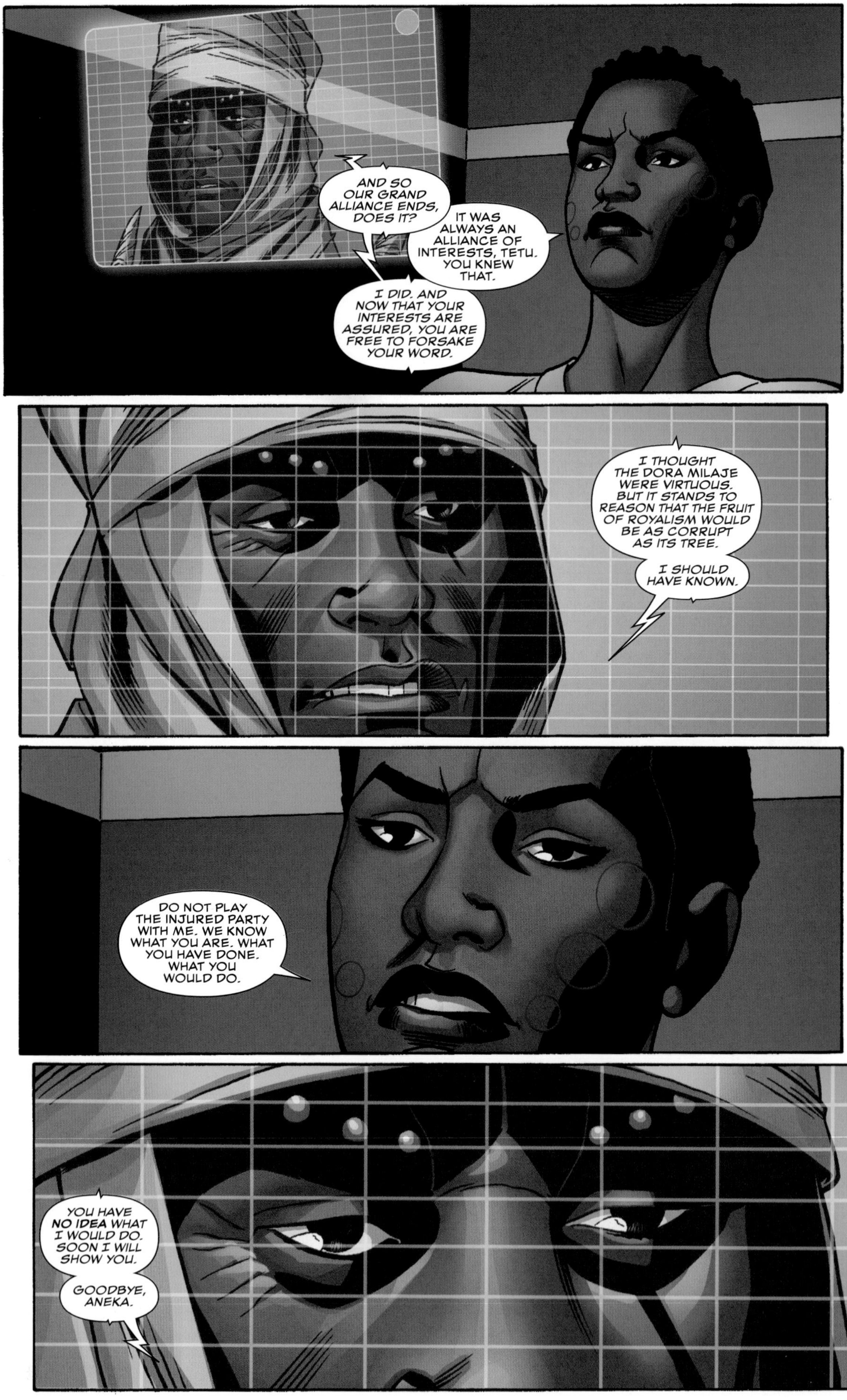

AND SO OUR GRAND ALLIANCE ENDS, DOES IT?
IT WAS ALWAYS AN ALLIANCE OF INTERESTS, TETU. YOU KNEW THAT.
I DID. AND NOW THAT YOUR INTERESTS ARE ASSURED, YOU ARE FREE TO FORSAKE YOUR WORD.
I THOUGHT THE DORA MILAJE WERE VIRTUOUS. BUT IT STANDS TO REASON THAT THE FRUIT OF ROYALISM WOULD BE AS CORRUPT AS ITS TREE.
I SHOULD HAVE KNOWN.
DO NOT PLAY THE INJURED PARTY WITH ME. WE KNOW WHAT YOU ARE. WHAT YOU HAVE DONE. WHAT YOU WOULD DO.
YOU HAVE **NO IDEA** WHAT I WOULD DO. SOON I WILL SHOW YOU.
GOODBYE, ANEKA.

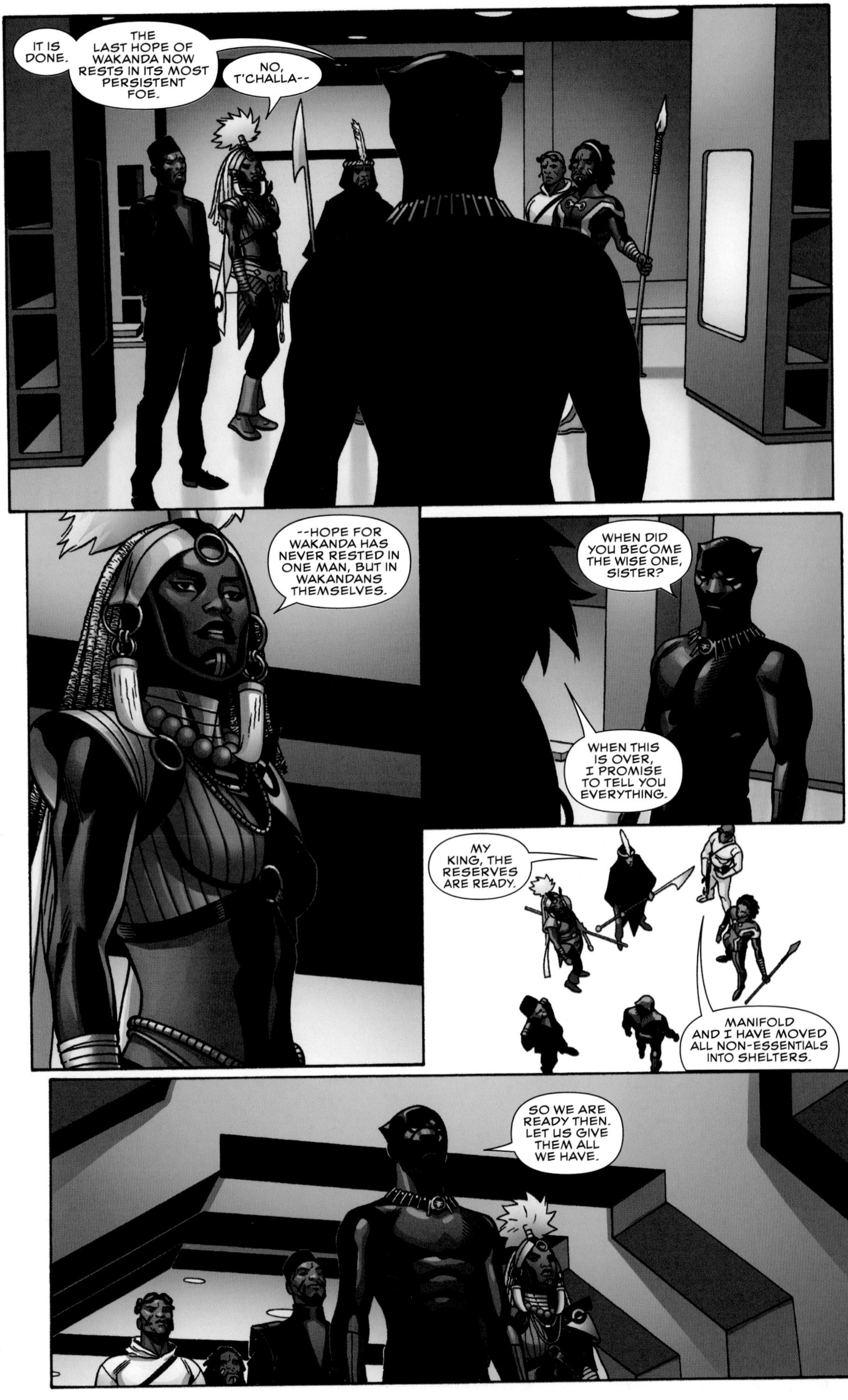
IT IS DONE.
THE LAST HOPE OF WAKANDA NOW RESTS IN ITS MOST PERSISTENT FOE.
NO, T'CHALLA--
--HOPE FOR WAKANDA HAS NEVER RESTED IN ONE MAN, BUT IN WAKANDANS THEMSELVES.
WHEN DID YOU BECOME THE WISE ONE, SISTER?
WHEN THIS IS OVER, I PROMISE TO TELL YOU EVERYTHING.
MY KING, THE RESERVES ARE READY.
MANIFOLD AND I HAVE MOVED ALL NON-ESSENTIALS INTO SHELTERS.
SO WE ARE READY THEN. LET US GIVE THEM ALL WE HAVE.

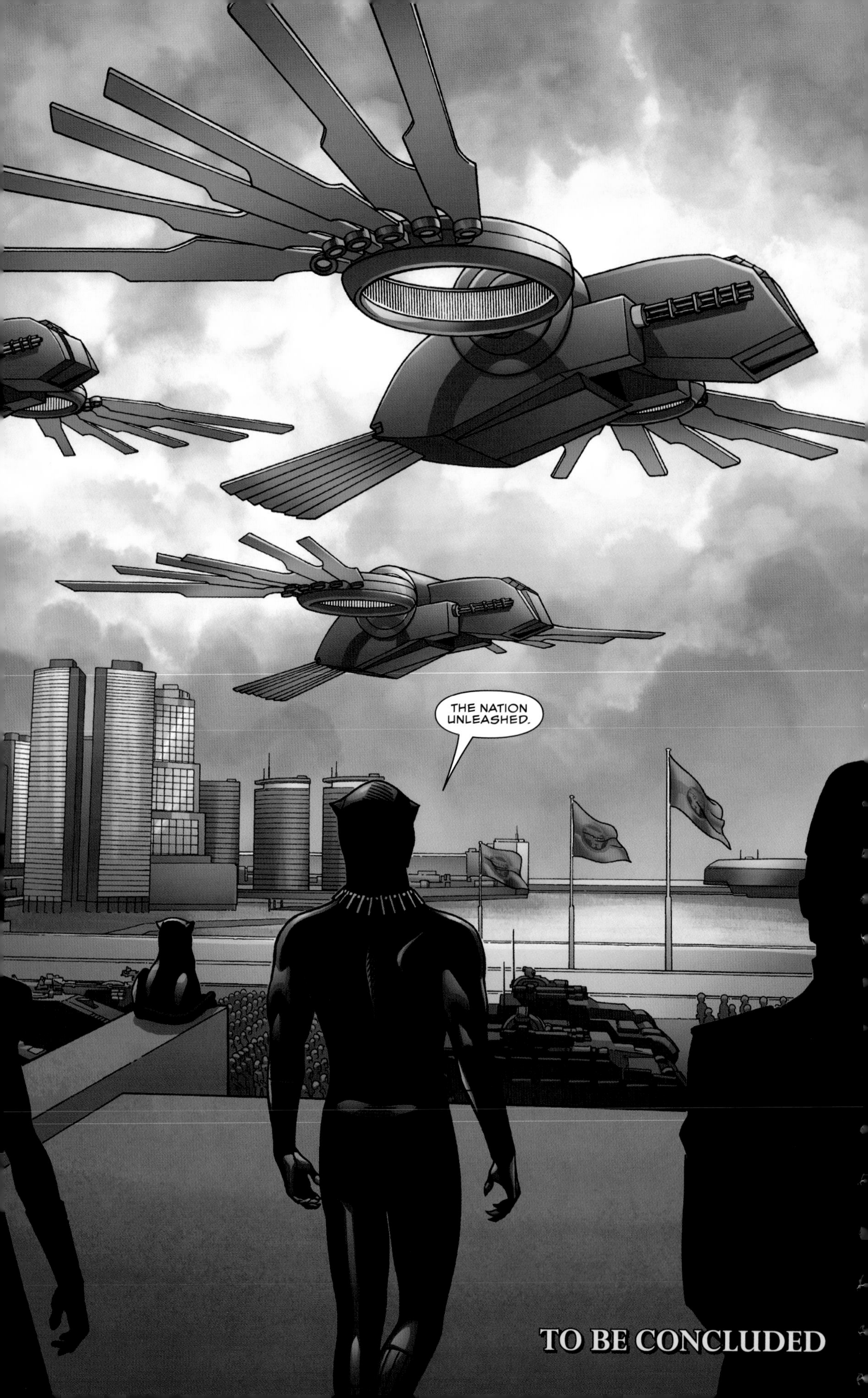
THE NATION UNLEASHED.
TO BE CONCLUDED